Lu...

Fairy Penguin

A Random House book
Published by Random House Australia Pty Ltd
Level 3, 100 Pacific Highway, North Sydney NSW 2060
www.randomhouse.com.au

First published by Random House Australia in 2013

Addresses for companies within the Random House Group can be found at
www.randomhouse.com.au/offices

National Library of Australia
Cataloguing-in-Publication Entry

Author: Murrell, Belinda
Title: Lulu Bell and the fairy penguin/Belinda Murrell; Serena Geddes, illustrator
ISBN: 978 1 74275 877 0 (pbk.)
Series: Murrell, Belinda. Lulu Bell; 2
Target audience: For primary school age
Subjects: Little blue penguin – Juvenile fiction
Other authors/contributors: Geddes, Serena
Dewey number: A823.4

Cover and internal illustrations by Serena Geddes
Cover design by Christabella Designs
Internal design and typesetting in 16/22 pt Bembo by Anna Warren, Warren Ventures
Printed in Australia by Griffin Press, an accredited ISO AS/NZS 14001:2004
Environmental Management System printer

Random House Australia uses papers that are natural, renewable and recyclable
products and made from wood grown in sustainable forests. The logging and
manufacturing processes are expected to conform to the environmental regulations
of the country of origin.

Lulu Bell and the Fairy Penguin

Belinda Murrell

Illustrated by Serena Geddes

RANDOM HOUSE AUSTRALIA

Molly   Tien and Sam   Lulu

Dad   Mum   Gus   Rosie

For Pippa Masson and Paul Macdonald, who encouraged me to create Lulu, and for Zoe Walton, Kimberley Bennett and Serena Geddes, who helped Lulu come alive.

Chapter 1

Pickles

It was Tuesday morning and the Bell family was getting ready for school. Lulu Bell looked closely at the tortoiseshell cat by her feet.

'Pickles is looking very round,' said Lulu. 'I think she might pop!'

'That's because she's going to have kittens any day now,' said Mum.

Pickles stared at Lulu and meowed. She wanted more breakfast. Lulu stroked

Pickles and rubbed her plump tummy.

Mum was making chicken-and-lettuce sandwiches. She dropped a chunk of chicken in the bowl for Pickles to gobble up.

Lulu's little sister Rosie was sitting on a stool at the bench. 'I wonder how many kittens Pickles will have?' she asked. 'Maybe she'll have twenty!'

Mum laughed. 'Dad thinks maybe four or five,' she replied. 'If Pickles were having twenty, she really would pop!'

Lulu's dad was a vet, and the family lived in the rambling house behind Shelly Beach Veterinary Hospital.

Lulu went to the pantry to get out

some cereal for breakfast. The box felt
very heavy. When Lulu shook it over her
bowl, a pile of plastic action figures fell
out.

'Oh no,' wailed Lulu. She checked
inside the box. 'There's no cereal left.'

The kitchen door flew open and in
darted a big brown dog. She was chased
by a tiny superhero. A pair of bright
brown eyes peered out from behind the
hero's black mask. He wore a cheeky
grin.

Lulu glared at her brother. 'Gus, did
you eat all the cereal?' she asked. She
waved the empty box and the handful of
toys.

The grin disappeared and Gus shook
his head. He pointed at the big dog
beside him.

'Jessie did,' said Gus.

Lulu wrinkled her
nose. 'How did Jessie get the cereal?'

Jessie slunk away and hid under the
table. Her ears drooped.

'Jessie naughty,' said Gus. He stuck his
thumb in his mouth.

'Do you mean you fed her the cereal,
Gus?' asked Lulu.

Gus zoomed off, his antennae
bobbing.

Mum smiled at Lulu. 'Never mind,
honey bun,' Mum said. 'I'll make you

some toast for breakfast. Rosie, why don't you read your home reader out loud to us while the bread toasts?'

While Rosie read from her homework book, Lulu worked on her latest drawing. She was making a book of flower fairy drawings. She had finished Fairy Rose and Fairy Daisy, and was now working on Fairy Lily.

'Lovely reading, Rosie. You are doing so well.'

Rosie glowed with pride at her mother's praise.

Mum brought the toast to the bench and buttered it.

'How's the drawing coming along, Lulu?' said Mum. She peered at the drawing upside down from the other side of the bench. 'I think the rose is my favourite fairy. I love the colour you've

used for her ball gown – blush pink with
a tinge of palest yellow.'

Mum was an artist, so she always
encouraged the girls to draw and paint.
Gus rarely sat still long enough to draw.

'Thanks, Mum,' replied Lulu. She
compared the three drawings. 'I don't
know whether to make the Fairy Lily's
skirt white or pink.'

'Why not orange?' suggested Mum.
'The colour of a tiger lily?'

Lulu picked out a bright orange pencil and looked at it closely. Mum was right. The orange was perfect. She carefully began to colour the skirt.

Lulu thought about school. Yesterday Miss Baxter had hinted that she had a surprise announcement for the class. She had warned them that she needed lots of good arty ideas today. Lulu loved doing art. And she especially loved surprises. What could the surprise possibly be?

Chapter 2

Down the Hill

While the girls munched their toast, Mum peeled two oranges. She cut up the fruit and put it in plastic snack containers.

The girls packed their lunches and homework into their schoolbags. They found their hats and were ready at last.

Lulu's best friend Molly was waiting out the front with her mum and her younger brother Sam. He had started school only two weeks before.

Molly stroked Asha's silky ears.

'Could I walk Asha, please, Chrissie?' she asked.

'Of course you can, Molly,' agreed Lulu's mum. 'Lulu can take Jessie.'

The group walked down the hill, chatting and laughing. Mum pushed Gus in the pram. A neighbour waved and called hello as they passed.

It was a fine morning, with a deep-blue sky. A flock of white-and-yellow cockatoos swooped overhead. They squawked and cawed.

'It's going to be scorching today,' said Mum. 'If it's still hot this afternoon, we might go to the beach for a swim. Would you, Molly and Sam like to come too, Tien?'

Molly's mum Tien nodded. 'What a lovely idea,' she said. 'We can take a picnic afternoon tea.'

'Yay,' cried Lulu, Rosie and Molly together. Sam smiled.

'Can we take our boogie boards?' asked Lulu.

'And my angel wings?' suggested Rosie.

'Why not?' replied Mum. 'It'll be fun. Perhaps we can have fish and chips for dinner on the beach.'

Jessie wagged her tail extra-fast. 'Dinner' was her favourite word.

'Woof?' the dog asked. She looked back and forth between Mum and Lulu.

'Not you, Jessie,' replied Mum. 'You and Asha are staying home.'

Jessie's tail drooped and her eyes stared up mournfully. Lulu patted her head.

'Never mind, girl,' said Lulu. 'We'll save you some chips.'

Jessie smiled happily again. She really was the smiliest dog in the world.

At the school gate, Mum kissed both of her girls and waved goodbye. Gus waved goodbye too.

'See you this afternoon. Have a lovely day,' called both mums.

'Bye, Mum. Love you, Mum,' called Lulu, Rosie, Sam and Molly.

'Love you, too.'

Now Lulu had *two* things to look forward to. First was Miss Baxter's surprise. Then there was the trip to the beach.

Chapter 3

After School

The summer sun blazed down when the bell rang for the end of school.

Some of the year six boys were having a water fight. They squirted each other with their water bottles. One of them squirted Lulu. She squealed with shock. The icy water felt lovely and cool down her back.

Lulu's mum and Molly's mum were waiting under the shade of a tree in the playground. Mum looked cool and calm in a blue floral sundress. Molly's brother Sam was standing close beside his mother.

Gus was wearing his Bug Boy suit despite the heat. He ran to the climbing frame with some friends from pre-school.

Lulu and Molly skipped over to meet their mothers. They dumped their school bags beside the pram. It was piled high with towels, beach bags, boogie boards and Rosie's angel wings.

'Hello there, honey bun,' said Mum. She gave Lulu a hug. 'How was your day?'

'It was great, Mum,' said Lulu.
'Guess what Miss Baxter's surprise was?
She has asked us all to draw a design
for a mural. Our class is going to do a
giant painting on the fence of a new
building site.'

Lulu's face shone with excitement.

'That sounds like fun,' said Mum. 'Do
you have any ideas for it yet?'

'I'm not sure,' replied Lulu. She
chewed her lip. 'Miss Baxter said that the
mural will be up for at least a year, so it
needs to be very special. At first I thought
about doing some flower fairies. But the
building company wants the mural to be
about our local community.'

'Well, perhaps you will get some
ideas down at the beach,' replied Mum.
'I thought we could go there straight
away. Where's Rosie?'

Lulu waved her hand towards the hall. Rosie was surrounded by a group of girls. They were all chatting and giggling.

'Bye, Ruby. Bye, Mia. See you tomorrow,' said Rosie. She ran towards her family. 'Hi, Mum. Did you remember my angel wings?'

'Right here, honey bun,' said Mum. She unhooked the feathery white wings from the back of the pram.

Rosie slipped the straps over her shoulders and twirled around happily.

'Come on, Gus,' called Mum. 'It's time to go to the beach for a swim.'

Gus ignored her and scrambled higher on the climbing frame. He perched on the top rung. A wicked smile spread across his face and he waved to all the children below.

Lulu tossed a plait over her shoulder.

'Shall I climb up and get him for you, Mum?' she offered.

'Thanks, honey bun,' replied Mum with a smile. 'It's too high for me.'

Lulu swung hand over hand up the rope net.

'Gussie. Time to come down,' she said.

'I not Gus, I Bug Boy,' insisted Gus. He scowled at his sister.

'I know,' coaxed Lulu. 'But it's time to go on an adventure at the beach. We can catch some crabs and build a huge sandcastle.'

Gus's eyes lit up behind his mask.

'Do you want to come for a slide on my boogie board?' offered Lulu. 'I'll pull you along.'

Gus nodded eagerly. Lulu held out her hand.

'Come on then, Bug Boy.'

Together they climbed down again to join Mum, Rosie, Molly, Sam and Tien.

'Thanks, honey bun,' said Mum. 'Let's go to the beach and see if we can find something to inspire your mural design.'

Chapter 4

Beach Fun

It was a five-minute walk from school to the sheltered cove beach. The sun danced on the blue water of the harbour. It glinted and glittered. Dazzling white sailboats skimmed across the water and a ferry honked its horn. Seagulls swooped and soared, squabbling for scraps. The air smelt of salt and seaweed and hot chips.

The two mums carried the pram and all the gear onto the yellow sand. Lulu pulled off her hot shoes and socks. She squelched the crumbly sand between her toes.

The mums made a screen of beach towels. The children took turns to duck behind the towels and wriggle into their swimming costumes and rash vests. Mum and Tien slathered them all with sunscreen.

'Race you in,' called Lulu. She threw her hat on her bag and set off towards the water.

Molly and Rosie squealed and chased her. They splashed through the tiny waves on the shore.

The water was cold and clear and wonderful. It washed away the stickiness of the day. The girls dived and dunked, catching each other by the heel.

Gus ran into the water, still wearing his Bug Boy costume. He wore his floaties over the top. He jumped into the shallows and shrieked with glee. Sam followed more slowly.

'Let's dive down to the bottom like mermaids and find shells,' suggested Rosie. 'Maybe we'll find a magical pearl.'

'Or a dolphin baby,' added Lulu.

The two mums dropped their sundresses onto the sand. They were already wearing their swimming costumes underneath. They swam out into the deep water and back. Then they sat on the beach, watching and chatting.

For afternoon tea, Mum had cut up

an icy cold watermelon and a juicy sweet pineapple, and added some pale green grapes. Everyone sat with their legs in the water as they shared the sticky, crunchy fruit.

'This pineapple is divine,' said Mum. 'It tastes of sunshine and summer.'

'*Mmmm,*' agreed Molly.

Lulu sucked a wedge of yellow pineapple and let the juice dribble down her throat.

'*Dulishus,*' said Gus, his mouth full of pink watermelon.

'*You're* delicious, Gus,' said Mum. She smiled at him fondly.

'I not *dulishus,*' said Gus seriously. 'I'm boy.'

Everyone laughed.

True to her word, Lulu put Gus on her boogie board. She charged up and

down the beach, skimming Gus along the
wet sand.

'Faster,' called Gus. 'Faster.'

When they tired of that game, the
children wandered along the shore. They
collected treasure in their hats: shells,
feathers, driftwood, twigs and sea glass
washed up by the tide.

Together the five children built a
huge fairy house in the sand. It had lots
of rooms, towers, fences and walkways.
Twigs and sticks were arranged to make
a bridge. Gus dug a deep fairy swimming

pool, showering sand everywhere. Sam surrounded it with gardens of seaweed.

The girls decorated the sand walls. They used pink-and-white shells and polished green sea glass. The towers were topped with feather flags.

'Look, Mum,' called Rosie. 'Do you like our fairy palace?'

'It's beautiful,' agreed Mum. 'I wish I could live in a palace like that.'

She pulled her camera from her bag and walked over.

'Come on, smile for the photo,' said Mum.

The children gathered around the sand sculpture. They smiled up at the camera.

'Gus, don't you want to be in the photo?' asked Mum.

Gus pouted, but then his eyes took on

a wicked glint. 'Bug Boy to the rescue,'
shouted Gus.

He stood up and took a running leap.
He landed right in the middle of the
fairy palace. It smashed to pieces. Sand
spattered all over everyone.

'*Gus,*' shouted Molly, Lulu and Rosie together.

'Oh, never mind, honey buns,' sighed Mum. 'I think it's time for another swim.'

They jumped in the water to wash off the sticky sand. Lulu and Molly had a boogie board race. They paddled out into the deep water and back. On the shore, Mum helped Sam, Rosie and Gus to build a new sandcastle.

Chapter 5

The Runaway Dog

The sun was sinking on the western horizon. It streaked the sky with brilliant hues of crimson, gold and purple.

Lulu, Rosie, Gus, Molly and Sam were exploring the rock pools. They peered at crabs and periwinkles. They poked at the sea anemones with their fingers to make them close up.

'Lulu,' called Mum. 'Rosie, Gus. It's time to leave. Let's go and buy some fish and chips for dinner.'

The mums packed up. The children
dried off and put on their school
uniforms. Their skin felt crusty with salt
and sand and fun.

'If we're very lucky we might see a
fairy penguin,' said Mum. 'They have a
colony in this cove. Their burrows are
at the foot of those cliffs and under the
wharf. They go out fishing all day and
come back at dusk.'

'We learned about the penguins at
school,' said Lulu. 'Miss Baxter said they
don't call them fairy penguins any more
– they call them little penguins.'

'I know,' said Mum. 'But I love the name fairy penguins. It seems to suit them.'

The group started walking towards the fish and chip shop on the wharf.

Lulu suddenly felt hungry. It had been a long afternoon of swimming, running and playing. Her tummy rumbled at the thought of crunchy, hot fish and salty, crispy chips. *Yum*.

'Look,' said Rosie. 'Is that a fairy penguin?'

Everyone craned their heads to see where Rosie was pointing. Among the dim shadows, the waves broke on the beach. A darker shadow was waddling up the sand.

'Yes,' cried Lulu. 'I think it is. Can we go down and look at it?'

'No, honey bun,' replied Mum.

'You can look from here. The penguins are wild animals. You need to stay well away or you'll frighten them. He's probably on his way home to feed a nest full of baby chicks.'

'Ooh,' cried Lulu. 'I'd like to see them.'

The five children clustered at the side of the footpath. The penguin waddled faster, heading away from the water.

A noise made Lulu look up. Coming towards them was a scruffy dog. It was running wildly and dragging a boy behind it.

Suddenly, the boy tripped on a bump in the footpath and sprawled face first on the ground.

He dropped the leash and the dog
bounded away. The boy started to cry.

'Lulu, see if you can catch that dog,'
called Mum. She hurried to help the
fallen boy. 'There now, sweetie, have you
hurt yourself?'

The boy had a
nasty graze on
his left knee.

He had more on his left elbow and on his chin. The grazes oozed blood, which made the boy cry louder.

The dog had jumped down onto the beach. It yapped with delight as it raced towards the little penguin.

Lulu and Molly sprinted down the stairs to the beach. The penguin waddled faster.

'Good dog,' coaxed Lulu. 'Come on, boy. Come here.'

The dog took no notice. It jumped on the penguin and knocked it over. The dog yapped and woofed. Then it tossed the penguin in the air with its snout.

'No,' screamed Lulu. She ran faster. 'Bad dog. Stop that at once.'

The penguin squeaked with terror. The dog picked the seabird up in its mouth and dropped it again like a toy.

Lulu reached the dog and grabbed its trailing lead. She dragged the dog away. The little penguin stayed huddled on the sand.

'Bad dog,' she cried. 'Molly, can you hold the dog for me, please?'

Molly took the lead. She strained to hold the bouncy dog back.

'He's strong!' complained Molly.

Lulu dropped to her knees in the sand. She was careful not to touch the little bird. It was breathing heavily. Tears filled her eyes so she could hardly see.

Mum came racing over. Rosie, Sam and Gus followed.

'Is it okay?' asked Mum.

'I don't know,' hiccuped Lulu.

The penguin was making low squeaking sounds. Lulu couldn't see any outward signs of injury. The dog yapped,

35

lurching and trying to escape.

'I think the penguin is in shock.'
Mum rummaged in her handbag and
pulled out her phone. She passed it to
Lulu. 'Lulu, can you call Dad, please?
Tell him what's happened and ask him to
come at once.'

Mum helped Molly pull the dog away
and made everyone stand back.

Lulu dialled her dad's number. Her
fingers were shaky.

'Hi, Dad,' said Lulu. Her voice
wobbled. 'It's me. We're down at the cove.
A dog attacked a little penguin. It might
be injured. Mum says can you come
straight away?'

'Of course, sweetie, I'm on my way.
Where exactly are you?' asked Dad.

The sound of Dad's familiar,
confident voice made Lulu feel better.

Dad would know what to do. Dad would make the penguin better.

'On the beach, near the wharf,' replied Lulu.

'Don't worry – just make sure no-one touches the penguin. I'll be there soon,' said Dad.

The rest of the group had gathered around Mum and the dog. There was Rosie, Gus, Molly, Sam, Molly's mum, the boy who'd fallen over and now his mother.

'Dad's coming,' said Lulu.

Mum brushed Lulu's hair back and kissed her on the forehead. 'Good work, honey bun,' said Mum. 'You've done well.'

'Scruffy, you bad, bad dog,' said the boy's mother. 'I can't think what came over him.' She looked at her son. 'Poor Finn, are you feeling better now?'

Finn still looked shaken, but his grazes had stopped bleeding. Scruffy looked dejected now. His tail was between his legs and his ears were down.

'My husband is a vet and he's on his way,' explained Mum. 'I think we should go up on the footpath and wait for him there. Lulu, perhaps you and Molly could wait here with the penguin. Make sure he stays safe.'

Molly and Lulu squatted on the damp sand. The penguin lay still, a dark hump on the paler sand. Lulu could see her mum up above the seawall. She was talking to the other mothers.

'It'll be okay, little fella,' murmured Lulu. 'My dad will be here soon.'

Chapter 6

Dad to the Rescue

In a few minutes, Lulu spied the familiar sight of her tall, gangly Dad. He was carrying his black medical bag and a cardboard box. Lulu ran towards him.

'Dad. Dad. It's over here,' called Lulu.

Dad swooped her up over his head and kissed her. 'That's my precious girl,' he said. 'Show me this little penguin of yours.'

Dad ran his hands carefully over the

penguin. He listened to its heartbeat with his stethoscope. Carefully, he lifted the bird. He wrapped it in an old towel and tucked it into the cardboard box.

'I think this little guy is coming home with us,' said Dad. He hoisted the box and tucked it under one arm. 'I'll give him a proper check at the vet hospital.'

'Do you think he'll be okay?' asked Lulu. Her voice wobbled again.

Dad gave her a squeeze with his free arm. 'I think he'll be fine,' he replied.

Lulu's dad had driven from the vet hospital to the beach. Mum had found the car and packed all the gear into the boot. Finn and his mother were waiting with Mum.

'I'm so sorry,' said Finn's mother. 'Will the penguin be all right?'

'I think so,' replied Dad. 'But he's a lucky bird. I'm glad that Lulu and Molly stopped the dog. In another few minutes the penguin could have been dead.'

Finn's mother looked upset.

'Scruffy's never done anything like this before,' she said. 'He's just so strong.'

'I'm sure Scruffy's a lovely dog,' said Dad. He gave the dog a pat. 'But as his

owner you need to
make sure he learns
good manners.

Perhaps you and
Finn should take
him to training
lessons. Then he
can learn how to
walk to heel.'

Finn looked up,
his eyes shining.

'That would be
great,' he said. 'Maybe I could teach him
some tricks too.'

'Rosie and I taught our dog Asha
how to roll over and play dead and how
to beg,' said Lulu.

'And Jessie helps vacuum the floor
after dinner,' added Rosie. 'She gobbles
up all the crumbs.'

'How did you teach her to roll over and play dead?' Finn asked Lulu.

Lulu laughed. 'She'll do anything for a treat. Come over to the vet hospital one day after school and I'll show you. It's easy to train a dog when you know how.'

Back home, Mum put Gussie in the bath. He was *still* wearing his Bug Boy suit. Then she prepared a quick meal of baked beans on toast. Fish and chips would have to wait for another day.

Lulu went with Dad through to the vet hospital. She wanted to help him look at the injured penguin more closely.

In the consulting room, Dad lifted the bird out of the box. The penguin yelped and flapped his dark flippers in protest.

His silver-grey eyes blinked rapidly in the bright light.

'He's a noisy little fellow,' said Dad. 'That's a good sign.'

Lulu smiled with relief.

'Look, Lulu,' said Dad. 'His back is blue-grey to make him hard to see from the sky. And his tummy is white. That's so he looks like foam from underneath the water. Isn't that clever?'

'It is,' agreed Lulu. 'He's really cute.'

Dad checked the bird closely. He moved its flippers gently and ran his hands over the feathers.

'Can you pass me that tube, please, sweetie? It's antibiotic ointment,' said Dad. 'There's a slight graze on his side.'

Lulu handed Dad the tube and he smeared the graze with ointment.

'Nothing's broken,' Dad decided, 'but I think he's suffering from shock and bruising. I'll give him a shot of antibiotics. Then we'll take him back to the cove and release him.'

'Oh, no,' said Lulu. 'Can't we keep him, at least for a few days?'

'Sweetie, this little guy probably has a mate. She will be worried about him. Plus she'll have a burrow full of little chicks. They will be hungry,' explained Dad. 'You know, if Scruffy had killed this penguin, all his chicks could have died as well. The chicks need one parent to stay and look after them.

45

The other parent goes out hunting for food.'

Lulu nodded. 'Then of course he needs to go home,' she agreed.

'Do you want to come with me to let him go?' asked Dad.

'Yes please, Dad. That would be great.'

'We'll need to check with Mum,' warned Dad.

Mum was reading with Gus and Rosie. They were all snuggled up together in Mum and Dad's bed,

with their heads resting on each of
Mum's shoulders. Gus was wearing fresh
Bug Boy pyjamas and Rosie was wearing
a long white nightdress. They smelt warm
and soapy.

'Mum, can I go with Dad to set the
penguin free?' asked Lulu.

Mum checked her watch. 'It's getting
late and you have school tomorrow,' she
objected.

'Please, Mum?' begged Lulu. 'It won't
take long and I promise I'll go straight to
bed when we get back.'

'Oh, all right then, honey bun,' agreed
Mum. 'You make sure the penguin gets
home safely.'

Chapter 7

Back to the Wild

Lulu held the box on her lap as Dad drove back to the cove. She could feel the penguin moving around inside. He squeaked and yelped. He smelt fishy.

Dad parked the car near the wharf and came around to open the door for Lulu. He lifted the box off her lap so she could climb out. The beach was completely dark now. Only the footpath was lit by streetlights.

'Dad, can I carry him, please?' she asked.

'Sure, sweetie. Just be careful not to drop him.'

Slowly and carefully, Lulu carried the box down the steps and onto the beach.

'I think we'll let him go right where you found him,' said Dad.

Lulu's eyes slowly adjusted to the darkness. Finally she could just see the scuff marks from the struggle in the damp sand. 'There!' she said.

Lulu knelt down and placed the box on the sand. Dad slowly turned the box on its side and opened the lid. The penguin paused for a moment. Then he scuttled out of the box. He ran up the sand towards his burrow under the jetty.

'Welcome home,' murmured Lulu. 'Sleep well, little penguin.'

'Let's go home and get you to bed,
little sweetie,' said Dad. He lifted Lulu up
and carried her on his shoulders, high,
high above the ground.

Chapter 8

Fishy Time

In the morning, Lulu slept in. She was tired after her late-night adventures. When she finally woke, Rosie was already up and dressed.

Lulu yawned and stretched and then she climbed out of bed. Her school uniform was lying on the floor. It was all salty and sandy from the day before. She went to the cupboard, but her clean uniform wasn't there.

'Mum, where's my uniform?' called Lulu. 'It's not hanging up.'

'I'm just ironing it,' replied Mum. Her voice came from the direction of the laundry. 'Can you please feed Pickles and Pepper? And ask Rosie to feed the rabbit?'

'Sure, Mum,' Lulu replied.

She padded out into the kitchen wearing her pyjamas. Sitting in the middle of the floor was Gus. His mask was pushed back off his face. Between his legs was a giant tin of chocolate Milo. He was eating great mouthfuls with a spoon. His face had a beard of sticky chocolate and the floor around him was sprinkled with brown dots.

'Gus!' cried Lulu. 'What are you doing? You're not allowed to eat that straight from the tin.'

At the sound of Lulu's voice, Jessie bounded into the kitchen. She was very happy to help clean up the mess. She licked the floor with her long pink tongue.

Lulu picked up the tin, found the lid, and returned it to the cupboard.

'Not Gussie,' insisted Gus. 'Jessie did it.'

Lulu tried hard not to laugh.

'Yes – Jessie is very naughty,' said Lulu. 'Come on, let's clean you up.'

Lulu went to the sink to get a cloth. She wiped Gus's face.

Jessie licked the brown sprinkles off Gus's Bug Boy suit.

Next, Lulu opened a tin of sardines to feed the two cats. Pepper, the ginger cat, came at once. She meowed and rubbed her back against Lulu's legs. She gobbled up her food straight away.

'Pickles. Pickles,' called Lulu. 'Fishy time.'

Pickles didn't come. Lulu searched all the usual spots – on her bed, under

the lavender bush, on the window seat, in Dad's shoe cupboard. Asha padded along beside her, her nose twitching.

'Pickles,' Lulu called again.

Rosie helped. Mum helped search as well.

Lulu went through to the vet hospital, even though Pickles didn't like visiting there.

'Kylie – have you seen Pickles?' Lulu asked the vet nurse.

'No,' replied Kylie. 'She's due to have kittens, isn't she? Perhaps she's run away to make a little nest for them.'

Lulu frowned. She looked out the front window of the waiting room. The vet hospital was on a busy road. If Pickles had escaped out there, she could be catnapped or run over by a car.

Kylie smiled at Lulu's anxious face.

'Don't worry,' Kylie said. 'We'll find her. I'll help you look.'

Lulu, Kylie, Rosie, Mum and Gus

looked in all the likely places again. They
tried lots of unlikely spots too. Jessie the
dog was keen to help. She sniffed under
the kitchen table and all around the base
of the fridge. But Pickles was nowhere to
be found.

'Do you think someone might have
opened the gate?' asked Lulu. She looked
at the high gate that separated the back
garden from the side street. 'Could Gus
have opened it?'

'Bug Boy didn't,' said Gus. 'Maybe
Jessie did?'

'Oh, no,' wailed Lulu. She rushed to check outside the gate. But there was no sign of Pickles. Where could she be?

Chapter 9

The Washing Machine

Lulu checked under Rosie's bed again. Pickles wasn't there.

'Come on, honey bun,' said Mum. 'It's getting late. Why don't you run and get dressed? I'm sure I can find Pickles while you're at school.'

'Okay, Mum.' Lulu dragged her feet. She was very worried about the tortoiseshell cat.

'And could you please put your dirty

uniform in the washing machine while I make your breakfast?' asked Mum. 'The load's all ready to go – just close the lid.'

Lulu quickly put on her fresh school dress and brushed her hair. She scooped the sandy uniform off the floor.

She carried it to the laundry and threw it into the open washing machine. Down slammed the lid.

Just for a second, Lulu heard a funny noise. Then came the sound of water filling the machine.

Lulu walked away, wondering about ideas for her mural design.

She thought about the funny noise again. It had been a mewling kind of sound. Why would the washing machine mewl?

Lulu stopped and turned. She raced back to the washing machine. She flung open the lid and the water stopped. She peered down. A loud meow came from inside.

There, nestled on the pile of dirty clothes, was a sodden Pickles. She was surrounded by six tiny, damp kittens.

'Mum, Mum,' yelled Lulu. 'I've found Pickles. She's had the kittens – *in* the washing machine!'

Mum came running. Rosie came running. Gus and Jessie came running.

'Oh, my goodness gracious me,' said Mum.

Pickles stared at them and meowed. She looked as if she wasn't quite sure how she felt. Annoyed at being wet? Or proud of how clever she was? Pride won.

'Yes, you clever puss,' said Mum. 'What beautiful babies you have.'

Mum set to work. She pulled a pile of old towels from the bottom of the linen cupboard. Lulu helped her to line a big wooden crate with newspaper and more towels.

A knock sounded on the front door. Rosie went to answer it and returned with Molly.

'Mum asked if it would be okay if I walked to school with you today,' said Molly. 'She has an early appointment at work.'

'Of course you can walk with us, Molly,' said Mum.

'Look, Molly,' squealed Lulu. 'Pickles has had kittens. They are just adorable.'

'*Doruble pussas,*' agreed Gus. He stood on tiptoe and tried to see into the top of the washing machine.

'Before we can leave for school, we have to move Pickles to a safer place,' said Mum.

Mum carefully picked up Pickles.

She wrapped her in a towel and placed her tenderly in the crate. Mum rubbed her softly to dry her. Pickles meowed. She wanted to be near her kittens.

'It's okay, Pickles,' said Lulu soothingly.

'Here's a towel for you, honey bun, and one for Molly,' said Mum. 'We're going to dry the kittens very, very gently. Then we'll put them in the box with Pickles. Be super careful not to drop them.'

The kittens had their eyes closed fast and their coats were sticky. Their little paws scrabbled at the towels. They mewled for their mother.

One by one, the kittens were stroked dry. Then they were placed in the crate with Pickles.

Molly held the tiniest kitten up to

her face and nuzzled its velvety black fur.

'It is so *sweet*,' she sighed. 'I wish we had a cat who could have kittens in our washing machine. I wish Mum would let me have any pet at all!'

'You could,' cried Lulu. 'Oh, Mum, couldn't Molly have one of the kittens? Couldn't you ask Molly's mum if she can have one?'

Molly gazed between Lulu and Mum. Her face glowed with hope and wonder.

Mum laughed. 'I can't promise that your mum will say yes, Molly. But I promise I will ask her what she thinks.'

'Yes!' screamed Lulu and Molly together.

'Thanks, Mum,' cried Lulu.

'Thanks, Chrissie,' said Molly. 'Oh, how exciting! What will I call her? Perhaps Sooty or Blackie. No, that's too boring. How about Petal or Petunia?'

'How about Cassie? Or Miffy?' suggested Rosie.

'Bug Boy!' cried Gus, with a cheeky grin.

'No way!' cried Lulu, Molly and Rosie together.

Chapter 10

The Design Contest

Molly and Lulu were a few minutes late
to class. Miss Baxter had already marked
the roll.

'Sorry we're late, Miss Baxter,' said
Lulu. 'But my cat Pickles went missing.
When I found her, she'd had kittens
in the washing machine. They nearly
drowned when I started the wash.
Luckily we saved them. We moved them
into a box in my bedroom.'

Miss Baxter smiled. 'That's all right, girls,' she said. 'I'm glad your cat is safe and sound. Now, take a seat. Today we are going to vote on our mural design.'

Lulu sat down. She felt a flutter of excitement in her stomach.

'The builders have just erected a timber fence around their building site on the main street,' explained Miss Baxter. 'This is where we will paint our mural. Hands up – does anyone have any ideas?'

A dozen hands shot up around the room.

'Yes, Ethan?' asked Miss Baxter.

'We could paint a giant pirate scene! It could have pirate ships and treasure chests, cutlasses and cannons, parrots and swashbuckling pirates.'

'Very good, Ethan. I like that idea.

And what do you think, Jade?' asked Miss
Baxter.

'We could paint a long scene of
Shelly Beach with surfers and swimmers.
We could do lifesavers and
sandcastles, sailboats with
white sails, seagulls and
dolphins frolicking in
the waves.'

Lulu stretched her
hand as high as she
could reach towards
the ceiling. Her
bottom lifted right
out of the chair.

'That would be lovely, Jade,' said Miss Baxter. 'I can imagine it as a colourful painting of our local area. And what is your idea, Lulu?'

Lulu sat up tall. She flicked one honey-coloured plait over her shoulder. She could see exactly how the mural would look.

'I think we should do a mural about the little penguins,' suggested Lulu. 'We could paint the beach at the cove and the wharf. There would be burrows filled with chicks and penguins waddling down to the water. And we could paint some of the dangers that threaten the penguins. Like dogs off their leads and pollution and boats.'

Lulu looked around the classroom at her friends.

'Molly and I rescued a little penguin

last night. It was being attacked by a
dog. It nearly died and then all its chicks
might have died as well. The mural could
show people what they can do to protect
our own little penguins.'

Miss Baxter nodded. 'You certainly
have been busy since yesterday afternoon,'
she said. 'I think that is a wonderful
idea too, Lulu. We could also include

some of Jade's ideas, such as seagulls and sandcastles.'

Miss Baxter began to hand out sheets of drawing paper.

'So, now I want you all to take some time to draw a design for the mural,' said the teacher. 'Draw whatever inspires you. When you are finished, we are all going to vote on the best design. The builder wants us to start work on the mural tomorrow. They are going to throw a party for us to celebrate when the mural is finished.'

The students set to work drawing their ideas for the mural. Lulu hummed under her breath as she worked. She sketched out her design. Then she began to add detail and colour.

When everyone had finished, the students walked around the classroom.

They admired the different designs and chatted about them all. Finally, each child wrote down the name of the person who had drawn their favourite design. They dropped their vote into a box on Miss Baxter's desk.

Miss Baxter counted up the votes. Lulu sat with her stomach twisted with nerves.

'And the winning designer is . . . Lulu,' announced Miss Baxter with a smile. 'Congratulations, Lulu. I think this mural will be gorgeous.'

Lulu clapped her hands together. It would be so exciting to see her very own design painted onto a big wall.

Chapter 11

Painting the Mural

The next day, the whole class wore painting clothes instead of school uniforms. The building company had supplied everything they needed. There were paintbrushes, rollers, water buckets and paint pots in a rainbow of colours. Mum had come along to help too.

Miss Baxter divided the class into groups of four. Each group got to work on a section of the fence. A few children rolled on the colours for the background. There were bright blues for the sea and sky, and golden yellows for the beach and sun.

Other children sketched in details:
penguin chicks, burrows, a wharf,
fishermen, families, seagulls, sandcastles,
sailboats, ferries and fish.

Lulu painted a cute little penguin in the foreground. He had a glossy blue-grey coat and a white tummy. Then she painted a big scruffy dog on a lead, running along with its owner.

Lulu stepped back and admired the figures.

'Beautiful job, Lulu,' said Mum. 'It looks *just* like Scruffy.'

It took two whole days to paint the mural. Then the workmen covered it up with a canvas screen.

Friday afternoon came. All the children and their families were invited to a special unveiling of the mural. A photographer from the local newspaper was there. So were the school principal and the Mayor. The students all wore their best school uniforms with hats and shiny shoes.

Molly, Sam and their mum stood with the Bell family.

The Mayor stepped up to the microphone. The photographer took some photos.

'Good afternoon, ladies, gentlemen, and children,' began the Mayor. 'This is a special afternoon. We are here to celebrate a wonderful piece of community artwork. It is a mural painted by some of the students of Shelly Beach Public School . . .'

Lulu looked around. Where was Dad? He had promised to come along. Perhaps there was an emergency at the surgery? Where could he be?

Mum squeezed her hand and smiled.

'I would like to welcome a very special guest,' said the Mayor. Everyone clapped.

A tall figure shuffled through the crowd. It was dressed in a penguin suit. The penguin character cavorted and capered. It waved its flippers and made squeaky penguin yelps. The children all laughed with glee.

'Please also welcome Lulu Bell. She is one of the students who designed the mural,' continued the Mayor. 'Please come up, Lulu.'

Lulu blushed. Everyone turned to look for her. She picked her way through the crowd and stood next to the Mayor.

'Hello, sweetie,' whispered the penguin character. The man dressed up as a penguin was Dad!

The penguin bowed. He took Lulu's hand and kissed it. Then he danced around and around in a circle with her. The penguin waddled from side to side.

The audience shrieked with laughter.

The Mayor gave a speech about responsibility and community. He spoke about working together to protect endangered animals.

At last it was the big moment. Lulu and Dad untied the ropes that held up the canvas screen. It dropped to the ground and revealed the long mural. The rich summer colours gleamed. The painted penguins looked very cute. Everyone clapped and cheered.

'Yay, Lulu,' cried Gus. He jumped up and down in his Bug Boy suit.

The photographer took lots of photos. Of the mural and all the children who painted it. Of Lulu perched up on Dad's shoulders. And of Miss Baxter shaking hands with the giant penguin.

When all the excitement was over, Dad took off his penguin head. The family walked around to the cove beach. Molly, Sam and their mum came too.

Dad bought fish and chips for everyone. They sat in the warm sand and ate the crunchy, hot fish and salty, crispy chips straight out of the paper.

'Yum!' said Lulu.

'*Dulishus,*' said Gus.

'What a lovely way to finish the day,' said Mum. 'A picnic at the beach.'

'What an action-packed week it's been,' said Dad. 'Penguin rescue, kittens in the washing machine and an official launch for the beautiful new mural.'

'Speaking of kittens . . .' said Molly. She turned to her mum. Her eyes were pleading. 'Can I, can we . . . please?'

'Get a kitten?' asked Sam.

Molly's mum looked at the hopeful faces of all the children.

'*Weeeeell,*' said Tien. 'Okay. But *you* have to look after her, Molly.'

'Hurray,' shouted Lulu, Molly and Rosie. They hugged each other and danced up and down. Sam hugged his mum.

'Of course I'll look after her,' cried Molly. Her eyes shone with excitement. 'I'll love her and feed her and she can sleep on my bed. Oh, thank you, Mum. Thank you, Chrissie.'

'Have you decided what to call her?' asked Lulu.

'Ebony-Lou,' said Molly with a grin. 'Ebony because she is black and Lou because Lulu saved her life.'

'I like it,' said Molly's mum.

'A beautiful kitten named after a beautiful girl,' said Mum.

82

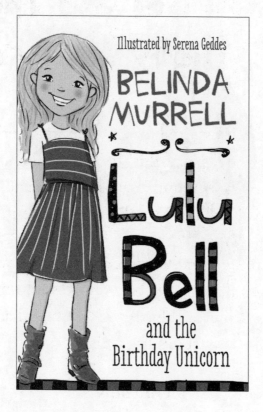

Illustrated by Serena Geddes

BELINDA
MURRELL

Lulu
Bell

and the
Birthday Unicorn

Lulu Bell and the Birthday Unicorn

It's almost time for Lulu's little sister's
birthday party. But there's a problem!
A pony is running loose and Lulu and her
dad, the local vet, have to rescue it.

Can they find the pony? And what will
happen if the naughty pony gets into more
mischief at the party? It's lucky that
Lulu has a plan!

Out now

Read all the Lulu Bell books

About the Author

Belinda Murrell grew up in a vet hospital and Lulu Bell is based on some of the adventures she shared with her own animals. After studying Literature at Macquarie University, Belinda worked as a travel journalist, editor and technical writer. A few years ago, she began to write stories for her own three children – Nick, Emily and Lachlan. Belinda's books include the Sun Sword fantasy trilogy, timeslip tales *The Locket of Dreams*, *The Ruby Talisman* and *The Ivory Rose*, and Australian historical tales *The Forgotten Pearl* and *The River Charm*.

www.belindamurrell.com.au

About the Illustrator

Serena Geddes spent six years working with a fabulously mad group of talented artists at Walt Disney Studios in Sydney before embarking on the path of picture book illustration in 2009. She works both traditionally and digitally and has illustrated eighteen books, ranging from picture books to board books to junior novels.

www.serenageddes.com.au

Loved the book?

There's so much more
stuff to check out online

AUSTRALIAN READERS:

randomhouse.com.au/kids

NEW ZEALAND READERS:

randomhouse.co.nz/kids